Fantastic Vegan Recipes for the Teen Cook

60 Incredible Recipes You Need to Try for
Good Health and a Better Planet

Fantastic Vegan Recipes for the Teen Cook

ELAINE SKLADAS

Creator of Wandering Chickpea

PAGE STREET
PUBLISHING CO.

Tofu and tempeh: Tofu and tempeh are a couple of my staple proteins. The majority of the recipes in this book call for extra-firm tofu, which has a dense, porous texture and mild flavor. This makes it ideal for baking, searing and marinating. Silken tofu has a soft, pudding-like consistency, so it's perfect for whipping into creamy sauces. Tempeh, on the other hand, is a fermented soy product with a stronger nutty flavor and compact texture. Just like tofu, tempeh is extremely versatile and protein-rich.

Legumes: From salads to stews to tacos, legumes are incredibly versatile, nutritious and delicious—if you know how to prepare them. You'll find that many of my recipes call for canned beans, which are packed in a thick, cloudy liquid. Unless otherwise indicated, always drain and rinse your beans in a colander to remove any unwanted flavors. This is especially important if you're using a brand with added salt.

Nuts and seeds: Not only are nuts and seeds loaded with essential nutrients, they're a delicious addition to just about any meal. Toasted pumpkin seeds and sunflower seeds make the best crunchy toppers for salads, grain bowls and baked goods, while tahini (sesame seed paste) is perfect for making creamy dressings and sauces. I'm allergic to all tree nuts (except for almonds) so I pretty much use them for everything! When a recipe calls for almond butter, feel free to swap in your favorite creamy nut butter or sunflower seed butter. However, keep in mind that due to a harmless chemical reaction, sunflower butter may turn your baked goods green!

Nondairy milk alternatives: Nowadays, there are dozens of plant-based milk options to choose from. I grew up drinking soy milk, so that's what I use for the majority of my recipes. When a recipe calls for nondairy milk, you can also use almond milk, oat milk or another type of plant milk. Just check the ingredients to make sure there aren't any added sweeteners or flavorings.

Other vegan products: While I mainly cook with whole, minimally processed foods, a few of my recipes do call for vegan alternatives to cheese, butter, yogurt and so on. Kite Hill® Greek-Style Yogurt is my go-to for creamy sauces and moist baked goods and their cream cheese is also a staple. For thick frosting, buttery crumbles and shortbreads, Earth Balance® Vegan Buttery Sticks are ideal. As for vegan cheese, there are many different options, so try a whole bunch to see what you like!

WEEKNIGHT WONDERS

As a recent high school graduate, I know that *busy* takes on a whole new meaning when you're trying to balance a demanding course load with extracurriculars, social events and maybe even a part-time job. Cooking yourself an elaborate dinner every single night probably isn't realistic, but I've found that taking the time to prepare and enjoy a nourishing meal once in a while is a great way to recharge after a long day. In this chapter, I'll introduce you to a few of the recipes I like to make when time is tight and it feels like I have way too much on my plate (but nothing to eat). These meals don't require much prep or hours bent over the stove, yet they still manage to deliver on flavor. Many recipes, such as my Roasted Red Pepper Pasta (page 23) or Smashed Chickpea Salad Grain Bowls (page 27) are ready to eat in under 30 minutes. Although other recipes may have a slightly longer cook time, I did my best to limit the hands-on portion so you can get some work done or just relax in the meantime.

NUTTY NOODLE AND TEMPEH LETTUCE WRAPS

I like to think of tempeh as tofu's weird cousin. She may be a little funky, but honestly, once you get to know her, she's so much fun! These noodle lettuce wraps are my favorite way to cook tempeh: torn into craggy bites, crisped in a pan and coated in a creamy, nutty sauce. Crisp Bibb lettuce is the perfect vehicle for saucy noodles and helps lighten the meal. I love the subtle sweetness of almond butter, but feel free to experiment with peanut butter or sunflower butter.

Makes 3 to 4 servings

6 oz (170 g) brown rice noodles (preferably pad thai noodles)

⅓ cup (85 g) creamy almond butter

¼ cup (60 ml) soy sauce

2 tbsp (30 ml) fresh lime juice

2 tbsp (30 ml) water

1 tbsp (15 ml) pure maple syrup

1 tbsp (6 g) grated fresh ginger

1 clove garlic, minced

1 tsp toasted sesame oil

1 tbsp (15 ml) heat-tolerant oil, such as avocado oil

1 (8-oz [230-g]) package tempeh, torn into bite-sized pieces

Bibb lettuce leaves, for serving

Chopped fresh cilantro, for serving

Place the noodles in a heat-safe container and cover completely with boiling water. Soak for about 15 minutes, or until they are tender and separate easily.

While the noodles soak, prepare the sauce: In a small bowl, whisk together the almond butter, soy sauce, lime juice, water, maple syrup, ginger, garlic and sesame oil until smooth and creamy. Set aside.

In a large skillet, heat the heat-tolerant oil over medium-high heat. When shimmering, add the tempeh crumbles in a single layer and cook for 2 to 3 minutes on each side, until golden brown and crispy.

Lower the heat to medium-low and add about one-quarter of the sauce to the pan. Sauté the tempeh for another minute or two to allow the sauce to coat the tempeh. Stir in the remaining sauce and drained rice noodles. Cook over low heat until warm. To serve, fill each lettuce cup with the noodle mixture and top with chopped cilantro.

BLACKENED TOFU
WITH PEPPERS AND GRITS

This Cajun-inspired sheet pan dinner features crispy bites of blackened tofu and a sweet blend of caramelized bell peppers and shallots. I don't call for vegan butter in many of my savory recipes, but when it comes to creamy corn grits, it's the only way to go! I tested full-fat coconut milk, olive oil, nutritional yeast and even vegan cream cheese, yet nothing compares to the silky smooth texture and savory flavor created by the vegan butter.

Makes 4 servings

Blackened Tofu and Peppers

1 (14-oz [400-g]) block
extra-firm tofu

¼ cup (60 ml) olive oil

1 tbsp (15 ml) pure maple syrup

2 tsp (5 g) smoked paprika

1½ tsp (4 g) dried thyme

1 tsp dried oregano

1 tsp ground cumin

½ tsp garlic powder

½ tsp cayenne pepper

Kosher salt

3 large shallots, sliced

2 bell peppers, seeded and thinly sliced

Drain and press the tofu for 30 minutes (see Tip).

Meanwhile, preheat the oven to 400°F (200°C), set to convection mode. Line a large sheet pan with parchment paper.

For the tofu and peppers, in a small bowl, whisk together the olive oil, maple syrup, smoked paprika, thyme, oregano, cumin, garlic powder, cayenne and salt.

Tear the pressed tofu block into 1-inch (2.5-cm) chunks. Spread the tofu on one side of the prepared sheet pan and add the shallots and peppers to the other side. Drizzle half of the oil mixture over the tofu and the other half over the veggies. Toss to combine, keeping the tofu and peppers separate.

Bake for 25 to 30 minutes, tossing at the 15-minute point, or until the tofu and peppers are caramelized. Remove from the oven and let everything cool on the sheet pan for a few minutes before serving to allow the tofu to crisp up.

(continued)

Grits

2 cups (475 ml) water

1 cup (240 ml) unsweetened nondairy milk

½ tsp kosher salt, plus more to taste

¾ cup (120 g) stone-ground corn grits

¼ cup (56 g) vegan butter

For Serving (optional)

Chopped green onions

Lime wedges

Meanwhile, make the grits: In a medium-sized saucepan, bring the water, nondairy milk and salt to a boil. Once boiling, add the grits and whisk constantly until thickened, 2 to 3 minutes. Lower the heat to low and simmer for another 5 minutes. Turn off the heat and stir in the vegan butter. Taste and add more salt, if needed.

Serve the blackened tofu and peppers over a bowl of grits with chopped green onions and a squeeze of lime juice (if using).

How to Press Tofu: *Pressing tofu is an important step in this recipe and many others in this book because it allows the tofu to absorb as much flavor as possible and retain its shape while cooking. It's super easy, too! Simply drain the tofu from the package and blot it dry with paper towels. I like to wrap the block in a layer of paper towels as well as a clean kitchen towel to absorb even more moisture. Next, place the wrapped tofu on an even surface, such as a countertop or sheet pan, then place a flat, heavy object on top. A cast-iron skillet or a couple of books will work great. Let the tofu press for 30 to 60 minutes, or until it feels considerably firmer.*

BAKED RICE PUTTANESCA WITH BASIL AIOLI

Baking your basmati rice is a foolproof way of achieving light and fluffy grains without ever having to turn on the stove. This dump-and-bake recipe is perfect for busy nights as it requires very little prep work and uses mainly pantry ingredients. The basil aioli is optional, but takes only a few minutes to make. Blending up chickpeas and aquafaba into a light, creamy sauce is a neat trick I learned from bean master Joe Yonan, and it really completes the meal.

Makes 4 to 5 servings

Baked Rice Puttanesca

1 pint (298 g) cherry tomatoes

1 small yellow onion, finely chopped

4 cloves garlic, thinly sliced

2 cinnamon sticks

2 strips lemon peel

1 tbsp (4 g) no salt-added pizza seasoning, store-bought or homemade (see Tip)

1 tsp organic cane sugar

¼ cup (60 ml) olive oil

1 (15-oz [425 g]) can chickpeas (see directions for draining and dividing)

1½ cups (270 g) uncooked basmati rice, rinsed well

½ cup (90 g) pitted black olives, roughly chopped or torn

3 tbsp (45 g) capers, drained

Kosher salt and freshly ground black pepper

2 cups (475 ml) boiling water

Preheat the oven to 425°F (220°C).

In a large, oven-safe lidded pot, combine the cherry tomatoes, onion, garlic, cinnamon sticks, lemon peels, pizza seasoning and sugar. Toss with the olive oil, then bake, covered, for 25 minutes.

Drain and rinse the chickpeas, setting aside ¼ cup (60 ml) of the liquid (aquafaba) and 2 tablespoons (20 g) of the chickpeas for the basil aioli.

Once the tomatoes have softened, stir in the chickpeas, rice, olives and capers, and season generously with salt and pepper. Add the boiling water, then cover the dish and return it to the oven for another 25 minutes.

(continued)

SMOKY WHITE BEAN TOMATO SOUP

When developing this recipe, I enlisted the help of my mom who has been making cozy soups from scratch for as long as I can remember. This one features a smoky blend of fire-roasted tomatoes, sweet smoked paprika and cannellini beans. It's simple, easy to make and perfect for the days when you want something warm and comforting, but still on the lighter side.

Makes 4 servings

2 tbsp (30 ml) olive oil

1 yellow onion, diced

2 cloves garlic, minced

2 tbsp (30 g) tomato paste

2 tsp (6 g) smoked paprika

1 tsp sugar

1 tsp kosher salt, plus more if needed

½ tsp fennel seeds, crushed

3 cups (720 ml) water

1 (15-oz [425-g]) can cannellini beans, drained and rinsed

1 (14.5-oz [410-g]) can fire-roasted tomatoes

4 celery ribs, chopped

2 cups (120 g) kale, roughly chopped, stems removed

1 tbsp (15 ml) sherry vinegar

Kosher salt and freshly ground black pepper

In a large, lidded pot, heat the olive oil over medium heat. When shimmering, add the onion and sauté for 5 to 7 minutes, or until softened. Add the garlic, tomato paste, smoked paprika, sugar, salt and fennel seeds. Cook for another 2 to 3 minutes, or until fragrant.

Pour in the water, cannellini beans and fire-roasted tomatoes. Bring everything to a boil, then lower the heat to a simmer. Add the celery and cook for 5 to 10 minutes, or until the celery has just softened.

Turn off the heat and stir in the kale and sherry vinegar. Season with salt and pepper to taste.

WEEKEND FEASTS

There are only a few things that I love more in this world than eating, but I fell in love with cooking when I learned to enjoy the process as well as the result. Although a quick one-pan meal certainly has a time and place on busy weeknights, my fondest memories revolve around the time spent preparing hearty meals surrounded by friends and family. If you have the time, cooking shouldn't feel like a rushed chore, but something that makes you happy. For me, it's standing over the stove, stirring a big pot of simmering Three-Bean Mole-Style Chili (page 54) or talking over the counter with my mom as the smell of Butternut Mac and Cheese (page 57) fills the kitchen. In this chapter, you'll find Sunday night–style dinners that even my meat-loving family has come to crave. While these recipes may take a bit more prep work and patience, they don't require any special skills. Many of them are fit to serve a crowd, but also make for fantastic leftovers. This way, a delicious weekend feast can easily become a quick meal on any day of the week.

SUN-DRIED TOMATO "MEATBALLS" WITH LEMON BASIL SPAGHETTI

Sun-dried tomatoes are my secret weapon for elevating any vegan "meat" dish. Tomatoes are naturally rich with umami and their dried, oil-marinated counterparts pack an even better savory punch. White beans and artichoke hearts help build a hearty base that's super satisfying and flavorful, yet still quite light and healthy. To balance it out, I like to enjoy these meatless meatballs over a big plate of lemony spaghetti with tons of freshly ground black pepper.

Makes 4 servings

1 tbsp (15 ml) olive oil, plus more as needed

½ small onion, finely chopped

1 small celery rib, minced

2 cloves garlic, minced

2 tsp (4 g) dried oregano

1 (15-oz [425-g]) can cannellini beans, drained and rinsed

¾ cup (174 g) marinated artichoke hearts, drained and finely chopped

½ cup (30 g) vegan panko bread crumbs

2 tbsp (30 g) oil-packed sun-dried tomatoes, minced

1 tbsp (15 g) white miso paste

2 tsp (10 ml) balsamic vinegar

Kosher salt and freshly ground black pepper

8 oz (225 g) dried spaghetti or other pasta shape

Zest of 1 lemon

Handful of fresh basil, chopped

Toasted vegan bread crumbs, for serving (optional)

In a nonstick skillet, heat the olive oil over medium heat. When shimmering, add the onion and celery. Sauté for 5 to 7 minutes, or until translucent. Add the garlic and oregano. Cook for another 2 to 3 minutes, or until fragrant.

Transfer the sautéed vegetables to a bowl along with the beans, artichoke hearts, bread crumbs, sun-dried tomatoes, miso and balsamic vinegar. Use a fork to mash until the mixture is mostly smooth; a little texture is okay. Season with salt and pepper to taste.

Use your hands to form the mixture into balls, about 3 tablespoons (45 g) each. Wipe out the nonstick skillet and return it to medium heat. Once the skillet is hot, add the meatballs and cook for 8 to 10 minutes, gently shaking the pan every few minutes, until they are browned and crispy on all sides. Turn off the heat and leave the meatballs in the skillet to keep warm until ready to serve.

For the lemon basil spaghetti, cook the spaghetti in generously salted water according to the package instructions. Drain and immediately toss with lemon zest, basil and a glug of olive oil. Season with pepper to taste.

GRILLED VEGETABLE PICNIC SANDWICHES

Nothing says summer like a loaded picnic sandwich! This one is piled high atop thick slices of sourdough bread with basil pesto, vegan cream cheese and smoky charred vegetables. I use a mixture of fresh zucchini, bell peppers and red onion for a satisfying blend of textures and flavors. If you're making sandwiches for lots of people, I recommend doubling or tripling the amount of grilled veggies but leaving the amount of pesto the same.

Makes 2 sandwiches, plus extra pesto

Basil Pesto
¼ cup (28 g) toasted almonds
2 cloves garlic
2 cups (40 g) fresh basil
1 cup (20 g) arugula
⅓ cup (80 ml) olive oil
2 tbsp (30 ml) fresh lemon juice
½ tsp kosher salt

Grilled Vegetables & Assembly
2 small zucchini
2 bell peppers
1 red onion
3 tbsp (45 ml) olive oil
1 tsp dried oregano
1 tsp dried thyme
Kosher salt and freshly ground black pepper
½ cup (115 g) vegan cream cheese
4 thick slices vegan sourdough bread

To make the pesto, in a high-speed blender, combine all the pesto ingredients, making sure the almonds and garlic cloves are on the bottom near the blade. Blend to a coarse paste, then set aside until ready to use.

Preheat an outdoor grill or a grill pan on the stove to medium heat.

For the vegetables, use a sharp knife to slice the zucchini lengthwise into ½-inch (1.3-cm)-thick strips. Quarter each bell pepper, removing the stem and seeds, then peel and slice the onion into ½-inch (1.3-cm)-thick rounds.

In a small bowl, stir together the olive oil, oregano and thyme. Brush the vegetables with the oil mixture and season generously with salt and black pepper. Grill the vegetables until tender and charred, flipping halfway through their respective cooking time. The zucchini will be done first at 7 to 9 minutes; and the peppers and onion should take 12 to 15 minutes.

Right when the peppers come off the grill, transfer them to a bowl and cover it with plastic wrap. Let the peppers steam for 10 minutes, then use your hands to peel off the skin. If you don't mind eating the skin, you can skip this step.

To assemble each sandwich, smear some vegan cream cheese on one slice of bread and top with the grilled vegetables. Spread a few spoonfuls of pesto on the other slice and put it all together. Slice and serve.

 Tip: Onions can be a little tricky to grill since they tend to break apart and fall through the grates of the grill. To prevent this, I recommend using a grill pan or basket.

ROASTING PAN RATATOUILLE WITH SOCCA

While a traditional French ratatouille can be quite labor intensive, this recipe lets the oven do all the work. It may seem like a shortcut, but you'll see that the richness and depth of flavor that arises from a few humble vegetables after a long roast truly makes this a magical dish. Speaking of magic, socca is super simple flatbread made from just chickpea flour, oil and water. You can do it the elegant way and tear off bits of socca to dip in your ratatouille, but I like wrapping up the pancakes like tortillas and making ratatouille-socca tacos!

Makes 6 servings

Ratatouille

1 large eggplant, cut into 1" (2.5-cm) cubes

½ cup (120 ml) olive oil, divided, plus more for serving

Kosher salt

2 large zucchini, cut into 1" (2.5-cm) cubes

1 large sweet onion, diced

2 bell peppers, chopped

5 cloves garlic, thinly sliced

⅓ cup (60 g) pitted kalamata olives, torn in half

1 (15-oz [425-g]) can crushed tomatoes

1 tbsp (5 g) dried oregano

1½ tsp (3 g) dried thyme

2 tbsp (30 ml) balsamic vinegar

Flaky sea salt, for serving

Fresh basil, for serving

Socca

1 cup (120 g) chickpea flour

1¼ cups (295 ml) water

2 tbsp (30 ml) olive oil, plus more as needed

¾ tsp kosher salt

Preheat the oven to 400°F (200°C).

In a large roasting pan or ceramic baking dish, toss the eggplant with 2 tablespoons (30 ml) of the olive oil and a generous pinch of salt.

Add the remaining vegetables to the pan along with the garlic, olives, crushed tomatoes, oregano, thyme, balsamic vinegar and another big pinch of salt. Drizzle with the remaining 6 tablespoons (90 ml) of olive oil and give everything a good stir.

Bake for 30 minutes, remove the pan from the oven and stir, then return the pan to the oven to bake for another 45 to 60 minutes. The vegetables should break down into an almost jammy consistency.

Right after the ratatouille goes in the oven, make the socca batter: In a medium-sized bowl, whisk together the chickpea flour, water, olive oil and salt until smooth. Set the batter aside to hydrate.

When the ratatouille finishes baking, preheat a nonstick skillet over medium heat for a few minutes. Add about ⅓ cup (80 ml) of batter to the skillet and cook for 2 to 3 minutes, or until lots of little bubbles appear on the top and the underside is deeply golden brown. Use a spatula to flip and allow the other side to cook for another 1 to 2 minutes. Transfer the socca pancake to a plate and repeat for the remaining batter.

Serve the ratatouille with flaky sea salt, fresh basil leaves and a drizzle of olive oil. Use the socca like a tortilla to make ratatouille tacos, or use it to sop up all the delicious roasting pan juices.

FARRO AND MUSHROOM RAGU

Although the ingredient list may seem lengthy, I promise that every single element helps make this vegan ragu one of my all-time favorite recipes. It's hearty, comforting and one of those meals that makes everyone question through mouthfuls of food: "This is vegan?!" Finely minced vegetables, chewy farro and sun-dried tomatoes make up the base, while a slurry of coconut cream, soy sauce and miso pack a flavor punch that puts your average meat sauce to shame. I like to mince the vegetables in a food processor to save time, but you can certainly do it by hand to practice your knife skills!

Makes 6 servings

¾ cup (90 g) pearled farro

1½ cups (355 ml) water

Kosher salt

½ large yellow onion

2 small carrots

1 celery rib

8 oz (225 g) cremini mushrooms, trimmed

3 cloves garlic

2 tbsp (30 ml) olive oil

2 tbsp (30 g) tomato paste

¼ cup (60 g) oil-packed sun-dried tomatoes + 1 tbsp (15 ml) oil from jar

1 tbsp (5 g) no-salt-added pizza seasoning, store-bought or homemade (page 37)

½ cup (120 ml) dry red wine

1 (15-oz [425-g]) can chopped tomatoes

½ cup (120 ml) low-sodium vegetable stock

In a large saucepan, bring the farro, water and a pinch of salt to a boil. Lower the heat to low and cook, covered, for 25 to 30 minutes. Once tender, drain off any excess liquid and set aside.

While the farro cooks, cut the onion, carrots, celery, mushrooms and garlic cloves into large chunks. Place in a food processor and pulse until finely chopped.

In a large, lidded skillet, heat the olive oil over medium-high heat. When shimmering, add the chopped vegetables. Cook, stirring only occasionally, for 5 to 7 minutes, or until most of the water has evaporated and little brown bits start sticking to the bottom of the pan.

Lower the heat to medium and stir in the tomato paste, sun-dried tomatoes and pizza seasoning. Toast for another 2 minutes. Deglaze the pan with the red wine and simmer for another minute or so to allow the alcohol to cook off. Pour in the chopped tomatoes and vegetable stock.

(continued)

¼ cup (60 g) coconut cream (solid layer from can of full-fat, unsweetened coconut milk)

1 tbsp (15 g) white miso paste

2 tbsp (30 ml) soy sauce

1 lb (455 g) short-cut pasta, such as fusilli

1 tbsp (15 ml) balsamic vinegar

Fresh basil for serving

In a small bowl, whisk together the coconut cream, miso, soy sauce and the oil from the jar of sun-dried tomatoes. Add the mixture to the pot along with the cooked farro. Bring everything up to a boil, then lower the heat to low and cover. Simmer for 15 minutes to allow the flavors to meld.

Meanwhile, cook the pasta in generously salted water according to the package instructions. Reserve ¼ cup (60 ml) of pasta water before draining.

Remove the ragu sauce from the heat and stir in the balsamic vinegar and reserved pasta water. Toss with the cooked pasta and serve warm with fresh basil.

HERBED OLIVE LENTIL BURGERS
WITH TZATZIKI

As a lifelong hamburger lover, I have high standards when it comes to veggie burgers. This recipe checks all the boxes, with a hearty base of caramelized mushrooms, rolled oats and tons of fresh green herbs. Kalamata olives and soy sauce add a meaty, savory twist that makes these burgers super satisfying, yet oddly addictive at the same time. A creamy Greek yogurt sauce called tzatziki tops off the dish and adds a delicious tang. For a lighter meal, skip the bun and go bowl style: Serve each patty over a bed of mixed greens with a tomato cucumber salad and generous dollops of that tzatziki sauce.

Makes 5 burgers

Lentil Burgers

2 tbsp (30 ml) olive oil, plus more as needed

½ yellow onion, diced

8 oz (225 g) cremini mushrooms, trimmed and sliced

2 cloves garlic, coarsely chopped

Kosher salt

1 cup (90 g) old-fashioned rolled oats

1¼ cups (250 g) cooked French green lentils

½ cup (30 g) mixed fresh herbs (parsley, cilantro, dill, mint, basil and/or chives), finely chopped

½ cup (90 g) pitted kalamata olives

1½ tbsp (25 ml) soy sauce

Preheat the oven to 400°F (200°C), preferably set to convection mode, and line a sheet pan with parchment paper.

For the burgers, in a skillet, heat the olive oil over medium heat. When shimmering, add the onion and sauté for 5 to 7 minutes, or until translucent. Add the mushrooms, garlic and a pinch of salt. Cook until the mushrooms begin to soften and release their moisture, about 5 minutes.

Place the oats in a food processor and blitz into a fine powder. Add the sautéed vegetables, cooked lentils, chopped fresh herbs, olives and soy sauce. Pulse until everything is well incorporated but not yet completely smooth.

Use well-oiled hands to form the mixture into five patties and place in a single layer on the prepared sheet pan. Brush the burgers with a light coating of olive oil and bake for 15 to 17 minutes (if you are not using a convection oven, flip them at around the 8-minute point), or until crisp around the edges. The burgers will continue to firm up as they cool, so remove from the oven and allow them to rest on the baking sheet for a few minutes before serving.

(continued)

Preheat the oven to 425°F (220°C) and line a sheet pan with parchment paper.

To make the tofu, drain and press the tofu for at least 30 minutes (see page 34). Then in a medium-sized bowl, whisk together the olive oil, cumin, paprika, coriander, turmeric, salt and sesame seeds. Tear the pressed tofu into 1-inch (2.5-cm) chunks and toss with the marinade. Spread on the prepared sheet pan and bake, tossing at about the 10-minute point, for 20 to 25 minutes, or until crispy. The tofu will continue to crisp up after it comes out of the oven, so remove from the oven and allow it to cool for a few minutes on the sheet pan before serving.

While the tofu bakes, make the sauces. For the zhoug, place all the zhoug ingredients in a food processor and pulse into a coarse paste. Season with salt to taste.

For the lemon tahini, in a small bowl, whisk together the tahini, lemon juice, maple syrup, garlic and salt. Add cold water by the tablespoon (15 ml) until the sauce loosens and becomes smooth.

To serve, stuff each pita with tofu and any desired toppings plus a generous drizzle of both sauces.

GREEK-STYLE BRAISED CHICKPEAS

These braised chickpeas are made with only a few simple ingredients, but don't be fooled—they're incredibly flavorful. If this were a traditional Greek recipe, the *revithia* would simmer in a clay pot on dying embers overnight so they'd be ready to eat after church the following day. In this version, dried chickpeas are soaked, then slowly cooked in the oven until they're melt-in-your-mouth tender. I like to serve them over rice or pasta with a fresh cucumber salad and Marinated Tofu Feta (page 118).

Serves 4–6

Braised Chickpeas

1 lb (455 g) dried chickpeas

1 large yellow onion, diced

⅓ cup (80 ml) olive oil

1 tsp aleppo pepper, or ¼ tsp crushed red pepper flakes

1½ tsp (4.2 g) kosher salt

1 unwaxed lemon, thinly sliced

Cucumber Salad

1 English cucumber, sliced

¼ cup (15 g) fresh dill, finely chopped

3 tbsp (45 ml) red wine vinegar

2 tbsp (8 g) fresh mint, finely chopped

1 tsp granulated sugar

Kosher salt

Freshly ground black pepper

Marinated Tofu Feta (page 118), for serving (optional)

Place the dried chickpeas in a large, lidded pot, such as a Dutch oven, and cover by about 2 inches (5 cm) of water. Bring to a rolling boil for 1 minute, then turn off the heat and cover the pot. Let the chickpeas soak for 1 hour.

Preheat the oven to 325°F (165°C).

Drain the soaked chickpeas and place them in a large baking dish or simply return to the pot if using a Dutch oven. Stir in the onion, olive oil, aleppo pepper and salt. Add enough water so the chickpeas are just covered by liquid.

Arrange the lemon slices on top and cover the dish with foil or a tight-fitting lid. Bake for 2 hours, then remove the foil and bake for another 10 to 20 minutes, or until the chickpeas are golden brown.

In the meantime, make the cucumber salad. Combine all the ingredients in a large mixing bowl and season with salt and pepper to taste. You can also make the cucumber salad ahead of time and marinate it in the refrigerator for up to 24 hours.

When the chickpeas are finished, serve warm with the cucumber salad and Marinated Tofu Feta (if using).

CORN TORTILLAS WITH AVOCADO AND SPICY MAPLE PEPITAS

Making your own tortillas may seem daunting, but it's actually quite easy and fun! The dough consists of just *masa harina* (a special type of corn flour), water and salt. If you live in the United States, you may have noticed how your typical store-bought corn tortilla tastes remarkably similar to cardboard. Homemade ones, however, are soft, chewy and full of flavor. They're perfect for tacos, but I like to let the tortilla shine with a simple filling of avocado, lime and these addictive crunchy pepitas. The key to keeping your corn tortillas soft and pliable is wrapping each in a clean towel as they come off the griddle.

Makes 4 servings

Spicy Maple Pepitas

½ cup (70 g) raw hulled pumpkin seeds

1 tbsp (15 ml) pure maple syrup

1 tsp avocado oil or olive oil

½ tsp smoked paprika

¼ tsp cayenne pepper

Corn Tortillas

½ tsp kosher salt

1 cup (128 g) masa harina (see Tip)

¾ cup (175 ml) warm water (90–110°F [32–43°C])

Preheat the oven to 325°F (165°C) and line a baking sheet with parchment paper.

To make the spicy maple pepitas, in a bowl, toss together the pumpkin seeds, maple syrup, oil and spices. Spread in an even layer on the prepared sheet pan and bake for 18 to 20 minutes, or until the pepitas are lightly browned. The seeds will still be quite sticky when they come out of the oven, so let them cool completely before breaking into clusters.

To make the tortilla dough, in a medium-sized bowl, stir together the salt and masa harina. Add the warm water and knead until a soft, springy dough forms (think Play-Doh®). If the dough seems a little dry or tough, add a splash of water. If it's sticking to your fingers, add a sprinkle of masa harina and continue kneading. Shape the dough into a ball and cover it with a clean damp towel to rest for 10 minutes.

(continued)

For Serving

1 ripe avocado, pitted, peeled and sliced

Flaky sea salt

Lime wedges

Once the dough has rested, divide it into seven or eight equal portions and roll each into a ball. Place a ball between two sheets of parchment paper, then press down with a heavy skillet to flatten the dough to about 1/8 inch (3 mm) thick. If you have a tortilla press, feel free to use that instead of a skillet.

Heat a cast-iron skillet over medium-high heat for 5 minutes. Once very hot, place a dough disk in the pan and cook for 30 to 60 seconds per side, or until speckled brown spots appear on the bottom. Immediately wrap the cooked tortillas in a clean (dry) towel so they stay soft and pliable.

To serve, top each tortilla with a few slices of avocado, spicy maple pepitas, flaky sea salt and a squeeze of lime juice.

Tip: Masa harina is a fine flour made from corn that's been treated with lime. Cornmeal, corn grits, corn flour and cornstarch are not suitable substitutes because they have different preparation processes, and therefore, different flavors and textures.

INDIAN BUTTER TOFU

This rich and creamy Indian-inspired curry is made extra special by a technique that changed the way I cook tofu. Freezing and thawing an entire block of extra-firm tofu makes it incredibly easy to remove moisture—without hours of pressing! Most important, the tofu takes on a chewier, spongy texture that allows it to absorb the flavors of the sauce without becoming soggy. If you're in a pinch, you can press the tofu for an hour instead of freezing, but know that it will have a much softer texture.

Makes 4 to 5 servings

Baked Tofu

2 (14-oz [400-g]) blocks extra-firm tofu, frozen and thawed (see Tip)

2 tbsp (30 ml) olive oil

2 tbsp (30 ml) fresh lemon juice

1 tsp kosher salt

2 tbsp (6 g) nutritional yeast

1½ tbsp (12 g) chickpea flour

1½ tsp (4 g) ground cumin

Coconut Butter Sauce

2 tbsp (28 g) vegan butter or (30 ml) olive oil

1 small yellow onion, finely chopped

¾ tsp kosher salt

Freeze and thaw the tofu, or press for 1 hour (see Tip).

For the tofu, preheat the oven to 400°F (200°C), set to convection mode, and line a sheet pan with parchment paper.

Use a few sheets of paper towel or a clean kitchen cloth to gently press any excess moisture from the thawed tofu blocks. Tear the tofu blocks into large, craggy pieces and spread on the prepared sheet pan.

Drizzle the tofu with the olive oil, lemon juice and salt. Use the edges of the parchment paper to gently toss the tofu. Now, sprinkle with the nutritional yeast, chickpea flour and cumin. Carefully toss once more until all the pieces are evenly coated. Bake for 25 to 28 minutes, until golden brown and crispy. Be careful not to overbake the tofu, or it will be too chewy.

While the tofu bakes, make the curry sauce, being sure you have all the ingredients ready to go before proceeding. In a large skillet, heat the vegan butter or olive oil over medium heat. When shimmering, add the onion and salt and cook for 5 to 7 minutes, or until softened.

(continued)

STREET CORN STUFFED POBLANOS

These loaded poblano peppers are roasted and stuffed with homemade refried black beans, brown rice and a creamy street corn salad inspired by Mexican *esquites*. I love this meal because it's filling, nutritious and, if you use fresh, sweet summer corn, absolutely brimming with flavor. Poblanos make for the perfect base because they're mild and have a thinner skin so they don't overwhelm the dish. I personally love the nuttiness and chewy texture of brown rice, but white rice, quinoa or any other cooked grain you happen to have on hand would also work well for the filling.

Makes 5 servings, plus extra corn salad

Street Corn Salad

3 ears fresh corn, shucked

1 tbsp (15 ml) avocado oil or other heat-tolerant oil

½ red onion, diced

1 jalapeño, seeded and minced

¼ cup (4 g) fresh cilantro, finely chopped

2 tbsp (28 g) vegan mayonnaise

2 tbsp (30 ml) fresh lime juice

1 tsp ground cumin

½ tsp mild chili powder

Kosher salt

Poblanos & Refried Beans

5 large poblano peppers

2 tbsp (30 ml) avocado oil

½ red onion, diced

3 cloves garlic, minced

1 (15-oz [425-g]) can black beans (do not drain)

1 cup (186 g) cooked brown rice or other grain

Preheat the oven to 375°F (190°C), set to convection mode. Line a sheet pan with parchment paper.

To make the street corn salad, use a sharp knife to remove the kernels from the cob. Heat a large cast-iron skillet over high heat. Once very hot, add the oil and corn. Cook for 5 to 7 minutes, tossing only once or twice, until the kernels are charred. Transfer to a bowl to cool while you prep the other ingredients. Once the corn has cooled off, stir in the remaining salad ingredients, seasoning with salt to taste.

For the poblanos, use a sharp paring knife to cut a wide opening along the side of each poblano pepper. Use your hands to dig out the ribs and seeds, trying your best to keep the rest of the pepper intact. Save the cut-out strips to use for the refried beans. Place the poblanos, cut side up, on the prepared sheet pan and bake for 15 minutes.

While the poblanos bake, make the refried beans: Chop up the remaining poblano strips and heat the oil over medium heat in the same skillet as you used to cook the corn. When shimmering, add the onion and poblanos. Cook for 5 to 7 minutes, or until softened. Add the garlic and cook for another 1 to 2 minutes, or until fragrant.

Drain about half of the liquid from the can of black beans and add to the skillet. Simmer for 5 minutes, then use the back of a spoon to crush some of the beans. Stir in the brown rice and season with salt to taste.

Fill each poblano pepper with the refried bean mixture. Return the sheet pan to the oven to bake for another 5 to 10 minutes, or until everything is heated through. Top each pepper with a few spoonfuls of the corn salad and serve.

LENTILS AND RICE
WITH CARAMELIZED ONIONS

This comforting lentils and rice dish borrows flavors and techniques from all over the Middle East. It's most reminiscent of *mujadara*, a signature Lebanese recipe made with caramelized onions, lentils, basmati rice and cumin. This version also draws inspiration from a Persian dish called *adas polo*, which has a bright blend of dried fruit and tons of fresh herbs. I also use French green lentils here because they hold their shape for a little textural variety. Similarly, the crushed pita chip topping is nowhere near authentic, but it adds the perfect salty crunch!

Makes 6 servings

¾ cup (135 g) dried French green lentils, rinsed

1 tsp kosher salt, plus more for cooking the lentils

3 tbsp (45 ml) olive oil

2 large sweet onions, thinly sliced

1 cup (180 g) uncooked basmati rice

6 pitted Medjool dates, chopped

¼ cup (40 g) golden raisins or chopped dried apricots

2 tsp (4 g) cumin seeds

1¾ cups (414 ml) water

1 cup (55 g) mixed fresh herbs (parsley, dill, mint and cilantro), finely chopped, divided

For Serving

Unsweetened nondairy yogurt

Pita chips (optional, but highly recommended)

Place the lentils in a medium-sized saucepan and cover with a few inches (about 5 cm) of water. Add a pinch of salt and bring to a boil. Lower the heat to low and simmer for 10 minutes. Drain and rinse the lentils with cold water to halt the cooking process. Set aside.

While the lentils simmer, get started on the caramelized onions: In a large, lidded pot, such as a Dutch oven, heat the olive oil over medium heat. When shimmering, add the sliced onions and 1 teaspoon of salt. Cook, stirring occasionally, for 20 to 25 minutes, or until deeply golden brown. If the onions start to burn at any point, add a splash of water to the pan and lower the heat slightly.

While you wait for the onions to cook, place the rice in a sieve and rinse with cold water, swishing it around, until the water runs clear. Set aside.

Once the onions have caramelized, add the dates, golden raisins, cumin seeds and drained, rinsed rice. Toast the rice, stirring frequently, for about 5 minutes, or until golden. Add the water, lentils, and half of the herbs, setting aside the rest of the herbs for serving. Bring to a boil, then lower the heat to low and cover. Cook undisturbed for 15 minutes, then turn off the heat and let the rice rest for 10 minutes before uncovering and fluffing with a fork.

Scatter the reserved herbs over the rice. Serve warm with a dollop of yogurt and a handful of crushed pita chips (if using).

CITRUS ROASTED CARROT SALAD

The best salads are not only flavorful, but also make the most of every ingredient involved. For this recipe, the carrots caramelize on a sheet pan along with a few sections of fresh citrus. The sweet juice of the roasted orange and lemon is then whisked in with creamy tahini and miso paste for the perfect salty-sweet dressing. Also, a word of advice: Hide those crunchy seed clusters from any lurking family members. They'll be gone before the salad's even on the table!

Makes 3 to 4 servings

Crunchy Seed Clusters

¼ cup (30 g) pumpkin seeds

¼ cup (30 g) sunflower seeds

2 tbsp (20 g) sesame seeds

2 tsp (10 ml) pure maple syrup

1 tsp olive oil

¼ tsp kosher salt

Roasted Carrot Salad

1½ lb (680 g) carrots, peeled and sliced into 3" (7.5-cm)-long spears

1 orange, quartered

1 lemon, halved

2 tbsp (30 ml) olive oil

1½ tsp (scant 4 g) ground cumin

Kosher salt and freshly ground black pepper

¼ cup (60 ml) tahini

1 tbsp (15 g) white miso paste

1 tsp pure maple syrup

Preheat the oven to 350°F (180°C) and line two sheet pans with parchment paper.

To make the crunchy seed clusters, toss together all the cluster ingredients on one prepared sheet pan and press them down into a single layer, using a spatula. Bake for 15 minutes, or until golden brown. Remove from the oven and let cool completely before breaking into pieces.

Increase the oven temperature to 400°F (200°C), preferably set to convection mode.

In a bowl, toss the carrots, orange and lemon sections with the olive oil and cumin. Season generously with salt and pepper. Spread the carrots on the second prepared sheet pan and bake for 20 to 25 minutes, or until the carrots are tender.

To make the dressing, squeeze as much juice as you can from the orange and lemon sections into a small bowl. Add the tahini, miso and maple syrup and whisk until thickened. Season with salt to taste.

(continued)

CITRUS ROASTED CARROT SALAD *(continued)*

1 bunch lacinato kale, chopped (see Tip)

Ripe avocado, for serving

Sliced oranges, for serving

To serve, massage the kale with the dressing and top each portion with roasted carrots, avocado, sliced oranges and a handful of crunchy seed clusters.

 Tip: Setting the oven to convection mode allows the carrots to crisp up and caramelize. If your oven does not have a convection setting, simply increase the temperature to 425°F (220°C) and toss the carrots and citrus at about the 10-minute point.

How to cut kale: *Rinse the kale under cold water and dry in a salad spinner or by blotting with paper towels. Holding the bottom of a stalk, strip the leaves from the stem. Roll up the leaves, then use a sharp chef's knife to slice into thin strips. You can either discard the stems or chop them up really finely to add to the salad.*

EMERALD SOBA NOODLE SALAD

Nothing makes me happier than a gorgeous green salad—especially when it has noodles! This salad is loaded with crunchy cucumbers, napa cabbage, edamame and a creamy almond butter–soy dressing. Soba noodles are the best in this salad because they're made from buckwheat, which has a nice nutty flavor. If you can't find soba noodles, ramen, udon or rice noodles will also work.

Makes 6 servings

Almond Butter Dressing

3 tbsp (45 ml) rice vinegar

3 tbsp (48 g) creamy almond butter or other nut/seed butter

1½ tbsp (25 ml) soy sauce

1 tbsp (15 ml) sesame oil, plus more as needed

1 tbsp (15 ml) pure maple syrup

Soba Noodle Salad

1 head napa cabbage, finely chopped

4 green onions (white and light green parts only), sliced

3 mini cucumbers, thinly sliced

½ cup (16 g) fresh cilantro, finely chopped

¼ cup (15 g) fresh mint, finely chopped

1 cup (150 g) shelled edamame, thawed if using frozen

6 oz (170 g) uncooked soba noodles

¼ cup (28 g) toasted almonds, roughly chopped

Sesame seeds, for garnish

To make the dressing, in a small bowl, whisk all the dressing ingredients together until smooth. Set aside until ready to use.

For the salad, combine the napa cabbage, green onions, cucumbers, cilantro, mint and edamame in a very large bowl. Cook the soba noodles in salted water according to the package instructions, then drain and rinse with cold water to halt the cooking process. Immediately toss the noodles with a drizzle of sesame oil to prevent sticking before adding to the salad.

Pour the dressing over the salad and toss to combine. Garnish each serving with a handful of toasted almonds and a sprinkle of sesame seeds. Serve chilled or at room temperature.

RICOTTA TWO WAYS

I couldn't decide which of these vegan ricotta recipes I prefer, so I decided to include both! The tofu-based ricotta is very creamy and has a nice tang—almost like cream cheese. It's the perfect protein-packed spread for crackers or a filling for Spinach Artichoke Quesadillas (page 24)! The almond-based ricotta, on the other hand, requires a high-speed blender and takes on a consistency that's more reminiscent of traditional ricotta. Add dollops of almond ricotta to a Caramelized Shallot and Wild Mushroom Pizza (page 58) or serve it as a base for Moroccan-Spiced Carrots with Chickpeas and Apricots (page 88).

Makes about 2 cups (500 g if tofu, 345 g if almond)

TOFU RICOTTA

1 (14-oz [400 g]) block extra-firm tofu, drained
¼ cup (60 ml) olive oil
1 tbsp (3 g) nutritional yeast
2 tbsp (30 ml) fresh lemon juice
1 tbsp (15 g) white miso paste
1 tsp pure maple syrup
¾ tsp kosher salt

Wrap the tofu in a few sheets of paper towel and squeeze out as much moisture as you can. Don't worry about it crumbling.

Place the tofu in a food processor along with the remaining ingredients. Blend until smooth, scraping down the sides as needed.

Use immediately or transfer to an airtight container and store in the fridge for 5 to 6 days.

ALMOND RICOTTA

2 cups (225 g) blanched slivered almonds
⅓ cup (80 ml) unsweetened almond milk
2 tbsp (30 ml) fresh lemon juice
2 tsp (10 g) white miso paste
1 tsp olive oil
¾ tsp kosher salt

Place the slivered almonds in a heat-safe bowl and cover completely with boiling water. Soak for at least 1 hour.

Drain the almonds and place them in a high-speed blender along with the remaining ingredients. Blend until smooth, scraping down the sides as needed. This may take several minutes of continuous blending.

Use immediately or transfer to an airtight container and store in the fridge for 5 to 6 days.

MARINATED TOFU FETA

This marinated tofu feta is a quick and easy way to add an extra burst of flavor to any meal! The texture and taste will improve as the tofu marinates, so I like to make a batch at the beginning of the week and keep it in the fridge to use as a topping for salads, grain bowls and pasta dishes. Try this tofu feta with a bowl of Roasted Red Pepper Pasta (page 23) or crumbled over Greek-Style Braised Chickpeas (page 77).

Makes 5 servings

1 (14-oz [400-g]) block extra-firm tofu, drained

¼ cup (60 ml) cider vinegar

¼ cup (60 ml) olive oil

3 tbsp (45 ml) fresh lemon juice

2 tbsp (30 g) white miso paste

2 tbsp (6 g) nutritional yeast

1 tsp pure maple syrup

1 tsp dried oregano

1 tsp dried thyme

½ tsp dried rosemary

½ tsp kosher salt

Wrap the tofu block in a few paper towels or a clean kitchen towel and gently squeeze out any excess moisture. Cut the block into 1-inch (2.5-cm) cubes.

In a wide, shallow container, whisk together the remaining ingredients until smooth. Add the tofu cubes and carefully flip them around a few times so each piece is coated in marinade. Let the tofu feta sit at room temperature for at least 1 hour and up to overnight in the fridge before serving.

BREAKFAST

In this chapter, you'll find my twist on indulgent breakfast classics like coffee cake, chocolate chip pancakes and the softest, gooiest cinnamon rolls you'll ever eat. For those of you who prefer a savory start to your day, I made sure to include a few wholesome options, like Green Herb and Zucchini Strata (page 125) or Savory Golden Porridge with Spiced Chickpeas (page 122). Whether you're looking for a quick school-day staple or a recipe to serve at your next special-occasion brunch, you're in the right place! And if big breakfasts aren't your thing, you can absolutely make these recipes for any meal. In all honesty, I prefer to start my morning with a rather boring bowl of microwaved oatmeal and enjoy my favorite breakfast foods later on. Some days, that means I'm having scrambled tofu for lunch, and other days, it's pancakes for dinner!

SAVORY GOLDEN PORRIDGE WITH SPICED CHICKPEAS

Although I do love a sweet stack of pancakes for breakfast, there is something nice about having something warm and savory as your first meal of the day. This turmeric-spiked golden porridge is made with thick-cut oats that yield a thicker, creamier oatmeal than your average rolled oats. The pan-toasted chickpeas add the perfect amount of crunch and flavor, along with crispy ginger and whole spices.

Makes 2 to 3 servings

Golden Porridge

1 tbsp (15 ml) olive oil

1 tbsp (15 g) grated fresh ginger

½ tsp ground turmeric

1 cup (80 g) thick-cut oats

2 cups (475 ml) water

1 cup (240 ml) full-fat, unsweetened coconut milk

1 tsp kosher salt

Spiced Chickpeas

2 tbsp (30 ml) olive oil

1 (15-oz [425-g]) can chickpeas, drained and rinsed

2 tbsp (30 g) peeled and roughly chopped fresh ginger

3 cloves garlic, thinly sliced

1 tsp cumin seeds

½ tsp ground turmeric

1 tbsp (8 g) sesame seeds

A big handful of baby spinach

Kosher salt

For the golden porridge, in a large saucepan, heat the olive oil over medium-low heat. When shimmering, add the ginger and turmeric. Cook for 2 to 3 minutes, or until fragrant.

Add the oats, water, coconut milk and salt. When measuring the coconut milk, aim for an equal amount of the solid cream and the liquid underneath. Bring everything to a boil, then lower the heat to low. Simmer, stirring occasionally, for 20 to 25 minutes. The oats should absorb most of the liquid and break down into a thick, creamy porridge.

Meanwhile, make the spiced chickpeas: In a nonstick pan, heat the olive oil over medium heat. When shimmering, add the chickpeas and cook, shaking the pan once in a while, until golden brown and crisp, about 8 minutes.

Next, stir in the ginger, garlic, cumin seeds, turmeric and sesame seeds. Fry for another 2 to 3 minutes, being careful to not let the heat creep up too high, so the garlic doesn't burn and become bitter.

Once the aromatics have crisped up, add a big handful of spinach, (or as much as you'd like) and a splash of water to the pan. Once the spinach has wilted, turn off the heat and season with salt to taste. Serve warm over bowls of golden porridge.

BLUEBERRY CARDAMOM COFFEE CAKE

I can't imagine that I need to convince anyone to eat cake for breakfast, but this blueberry coffee cake really is the best Sunday morning treat. It's loaded with bursting bites of fresh blueberries and topped with a crunchy cinnamon streusel. Nondairy yogurt is the key to keeping the cardamom-scented crumb moist, and while the vanilla glaze is optional, it does make this indulgent breakfast extra special. I know it might be hard to wait, but make sure you let the cake cool completely before glazing and slicing, to give the streusel time to crisp up.

Makes 9 servings

Streusel Topping

½ cup (112 g) vegan butter, softened, plus extra for the pan

¾ cup (90 g) all-purpose flour

½ cup (112 g) light or dark brown sugar

2 tbsp (24 g) organic cane sugar

1 tsp ground cinnamon

Cake Batter

1¾ cups (210 g) all-purpose flour

1 tsp baking soda

1 tsp ground cardamom

½ tsp kosher salt

1 cup (240 ml) plain unsweetened nondairy yogurt

¾ cup (150 g) organic cane sugar

⅓ cup (80 ml) vegetable oil

1 tsp vanilla extract

1½ cups (225 g) fresh blueberries

Vanilla Glaze (optional)

½ cup (60 g) powdered sugar

1 tbsp (15 ml) nondairy milk

1 tsp vanilla extract

Preheat the oven to 350°F (180°C). Grease an 8-inch (20-cm) square baking dish with vegan butter and line with parchment paper.

To make the streusel topping, in a small bowl, use a fork to combine the vegan butter, flour, sugars and cinnamon until the mixture resembles small pebbles. Place the streusel in the fridge to chill.

To make the cake batter, in a large bowl, whisk together the flour, baking soda, cardamom and salt.

In a medium-sized bowl, beat together the yogurt, sugar, oil and vanilla. Add the wet ingredients to the dry and use a spatula to mix until just combined. Fold in the blueberries.

Pour the batter into the prepared baking dish and use a spatula to smooth it into an even layer. Sprinkle the streusel mixture on top and bake for 45 to 50 minutes, or until the top is golden brown and a cake tester comes out clean. Remove from the oven and let the cake cool in the pan for at least 30 minutes before slicing.

To make the glaze, in a small bowl, whisk together the powdered sugar, milk and vanilla until smooth. Drizzle over the cake a few minutes before serving.

CHAI-SPICED CINNAMON ROLLS

Cinnamon rolls are a Christmas morning tradition in my family and they also happen to be one of the first desserts I learned how to make. With their irresistibly soft and gooey texture, chai-spiced filling and maple glaze, these ones are sure to impress even the nonvegan crowd!

Makes 9 cinnamon rolls

Cinnamon Roll Dough

1 cup + 2 tbsp (270 ml) water

2 tbsp (25 g) organic cane sugar

1 tsp active dry yeast

3 cups (375 g) all-purpose flour, plus more as needed

½ tsp kosher salt

6 tbsp (84 g) vegan butter, melted

Olive oil, for bowl

Filling

½ cup (112 g) vegan butter, softened

1 cup (225 g) light or dark brown sugar

1 tbsp (8 g) ground cinnamon

1 tsp ground cardamom

½ tsp ground ginger

½ tsp ground allspice

Vegan butter, for baking dish

Maple Glaze

1 cup (120 g) powdered sugar

¼ cup (60 ml) pure maple syrup

1 tsp vanilla extract

1 to 2 tbsp (15 to 30 ml) nondairy milk

Heat the water in a microwave-safe bowl in a microwave or in a small saucepan over the stove until it's lukewarm but not yet hot (110 to 115°F [43 to 46°C]). Stir in the sugar and yeast. Let the mixture stand for 5 minutes until the yeast foams.

In a large bowl, whisk together the flour and salt. Pour in the melted vegan butter and the yeast mixture and mix with a wooden spoon until a shaggy dough forms. Turn out the dough onto a clean work surface and knead for 5 to 6 minutes, or until soft and springy. If the dough feels too dry, wet your hands with a little warm water and continue kneading. If it's sticking to your fingers, add a dusting of flour, but err on the side of a stickier dough.

Place the dough in a well-oiled bowl and turn the dough over a couple of times so it's coated with oil. Cover the bowl with a clean, damp towel and place in a warm spot to rise for 1½ hours, or until the dough has doubled in size (see Tip).

While the dough rises, make the filling: In a small bowl, use a spatula to mix the vegan butter, brown sugar, cinnamon, cardamom, ginger and allspice into a spreadable paste.

Grease a 9 x 13–inch (23 x 33–cm) baking dish with vegan butter and line with parchment paper, leaving a slight overhang for easy removal.

Once the dough has risen, roll it into a 12 x 18–inch (30 x 45–cm) rectangle. Spread the filling mixture over the surface and, starting from the wider end of the rectangle, roll the dough into a tight log. Use a sharp knife or a clean length of dental floss to cut the log into nine equal-sized pieces.

In the prepared baking dish, arrange the rolls, cut side down, in a single layer. They will rise quite a bit, so each roll should just barely be touching the others. Cover the dish with plastic wrap and place in a warm spot to rise for another 45 minutes.

When ready to bake, preheat the oven to 350°F (180°C). Uncover the cinnamon rolls and bake for 30 to 35 minutes, or until the tops are lightly golden brown. Be careful not to overbake, these taste best when they're still a little gooey.

While the cinnamon rolls bake, make the glaze: In a small bowl, whisk together the powdered sugar, maple syrup, vanilla and 1 tablespoon (15 ml) of nondairy milk. If the glaze seems too thick, add another splash of milk until it's smooth and pourable.

Remove the cinnamon rolls from the oven and allow to cool for 5 to 10 minutes before pouring the glaze on top. Serve warm.

Tips:

While the dough is rising, fill a large dish with hot water and place it next to the bowl in the oven. Don't turn the oven on! The warm, moist environment will help the dough double in size. Be sure to remove the bowl of water before baking the rolls.

If you plan on having these cinnamon rolls for breakfast or brunch, you can roll out the dough the day before and let them do their final proof in the fridge overnight. The next morning, let the rolls come to room temperature and bake as instructed.

WHOLE WHEAT PUMPKIN MUFFINS

There's nothing like a warm pumpkin muffin on a chilly fall day, but you certainly don't have to wait until October to enjoy this recipe! Canned pumpkin puree keeps the whole wheat crumb perfectly moist while a sprinkle of raw sugar makes the tops so irresistibly sweet and crunchy. While we were growing up, we would always keep a batch of muffins in the freezer for a quick breakfast before school. If you're craving something sweeter, try adding semisweet chocolate chips to the batter!

Makes 12 muffins

2 cups (240 g) white whole wheat flour

1 tsp baking powder

1 tsp baking soda

1 tsp ground cinnamon

½ tsp kosher salt

1 (15-oz [425-g]) can pure pumpkin puree

¾ cup (170 g) packed dark brown sugar

½ cup (115 g) unsweetened applesauce

½ cup (120 ml) vegetable oil

1 tsp vanilla extract

Raw sugar, for topping (optional)

Preheat the oven to 425°F (220°C) and line a standard 12-count muffin tin with cupcake wrappers.

In a large bowl, whisk together the flour, baking powder, baking soda, cinnamon and salt. In another large bowl, beat together the pumpkin puree, brown sugar, applesauce, vegetable oil and vanilla until smooth.

Fold the wet ingredients into the dry until just combined. Use a large cookie scoop to spoon the batter into the muffin tin, filling each cup a little past the top. Sprinkle a little raw sugar on top.

Bake for 7 minutes at 425°F (220°C), then reduce the temperature to 350°F (180°C) and continue to bake for another 10 to 12 minutes, or until a toothpick inserted into the center of a muffin comes out clean. Remove from the oven and, as soon as the muffins are cool enough to handle, transfer to a wire rack to cool for 10 minutes before serving.

 Tip: Starting off the muffins at a high temperature and decreasing it partway through baking encourages the tops to dome, creating perfect bakery-style muffin tops.

CORNBREAD PEACH CRUMBLE

Fruit crumbles are one of my favorite desserts to make because they're easy, delicious and loved by all. This summery peach crumble is overflowing with a jammy sweet peach filling and a buttery cornbread streusel topping. For the sake of convenience and flavor, I use frozen peaches that are already pitted and sliced. Make sure you use finely ground cornmeal or masa harina for the crumble, as anything too coarse will have an unpleasant gritty texture.

Makes 5 servings

Peach Filling

2 lb (900 g) frozen sliced peaches (about 6 cups)

2 tbsp (24 g) organic cane sugar

2 tbsp (16 g) cornstarch

1 tbsp (15 ml) fresh lemon juice

1 tsp vanilla extract

Crumble Topping

½ cup (112 g) vegan butter, softened

½ cup (112 g) light or dark brown sugar

¼ cup (50 g) organic cane sugar

½ cup (60 g) all-purpose flour

½ cup (70 g) fine cornmeal or masa harina

1 tsp baking powder

1 tsp ground cinnamon

½ tsp kosher salt

Raw sugar, for sprinkling (optional)

Vegan vanilla ice cream, for serving

Preheat the oven to 350°F (180°C).

If the frozen peaches have developed a layer of frost, give them a quick rinse and set aside to thaw while you make the topping.

For the topping, in a medium-sized bowl, combine the vegan butter, sugars, flour, cornmeal, baking powder, cinnamon and salt. Use a fork or your fingers to work the mixture into small pebbles.

Place the frozen peaches in a large baking dish and toss with the sugar, cornstarch, lemon juice and vanilla extract. Top with the crumble and a sprinkle of raw sugar.

Bake for 50 to 55 minutes, or until the filling is bubbling around the edges. If the top starts to brown too quickly, tent the dish with foil. Remove from the oven and let the crumble sit for at least 15 minutes before serving with vegan vanilla ice cream.

LEMON POPPY SEED SNACK CAKE

Good news, folks: It's now totally acceptable to eat a slice of cake for a snack. This simple cake is exactly what I'm reaching for to satisfy sweet cravings throughout the day. Coconut cream and olive oil keep the crumb light and moist, while a simple lemon glaze helps tie everything together. It's quick and flavorful, but not over-the-top decadent. So, in other words, perfectly snackable!

Makes 9 servings

Lemon Poppy Seed Cake

Vegan butter, for pan

1½ cups (180 g) all-purpose flour

1 tbsp (9 g) poppy seeds

1 tsp baking powder

½ tsp baking soda

½ tsp kosher salt

¾ cup (150 g) organic cane sugar

¾ cup (175 ml) full-fat, unsweetened coconut milk

¼ cup (60 ml) olive oil

1 tbsp (6 g) lemon zest

3 tbsp (45 ml) fresh lemon juice

1 tsp vanilla extract

Lemon Glaze

1 cup (120 g) powdered sugar

2 to 3 tbsp (30 to 45 ml) nondairy milk

1 tbsp (6 g) lemon zest

Preheat the oven to 350°F (180°C). Grease an 8-inch (20-cm) square baking pan with vegan butter and line with parchment paper, leaving a slight overhang on opposite sides, for easy removal.

In a large bowl, whisk together the flour, poppy seeds, baking powder, baking soda and salt. In a medium-sized bowl, beat together the sugar, coconut milk, olive oil, lemon zest and juice and vanilla until smooth. If there are still a few solid flecks of coconut cream, that's okay.

Fold the wet ingredients with the dry until just combined. Be careful not to overmix. Pour the batter into the prepared baking pan and bake for 27 to 30 minutes, or until a toothpick inserted into the center comes out clean. Remove from the oven and let the cake cool completely before glazing.

To make the glaze, in a small bowl, whisk together the powdered sugar, 2 tablespoons (30 ml) of the nondairy milk and the lemon zest. If the glaze is still too stiff, add another tablespoon (15 ml) of nondairy milk until the glaze reaches a pourable consistency.

Spread the glaze over the cooled cake and let it sit for a few minutes to set before slicing.

 Tip: For a perfectly level cake, please use a metal baking pan. I've found that other materials, such as glass, cause the cake to sink in the center while the edges dry out.

TAHINI DATE BANANA BREAD

I feel like no matter how many bananas I eat throughout the week, there's always a few gnarly blackened ones left on the counter. An absolute win in my book! In fact, I have such an adoration for banana bread that I make it on my birthday every year, instead of cake. Of all the variations I've tried, this one, hands down, is the best. It's incredibly soft and moist, with chewy bites of Medjool dates, nutty tahini and a crunchy sesame seed crust. Top it off with a pinch of flaky sea salt and . . . good luck stopping at one slice.

Makes 8 servings

Vegan butter, for pan

1¾ cups (210 g) all-purpose flour

1 tsp ground cinnamon

¾ tsp baking powder

¾ tsp baking soda

½ tsp kosher salt

1¼ cups (375 g) mashed overripe banana

½ cup (120 ml) olive oil

¼ cup (60 ml) nondairy milk

½ cup (112 g) dark brown sugar

¼ cup (50 g) organic cane sugar

3 tbsp (45 g) tahini

1 tsp vanilla extract

12 Medjool dates, pitted and chopped

Sesame seeds, for topping

Flaky sea salt, for topping

Preheat the oven to 350°F (180°C). Grease an 8 x 4–inch (20 x 10–cm) loaf pan with vegan butter and line with parchment paper, leaving a slight overhang for easy removal.

In a large bowl, whisk together the flour, cinnamon, baking powder, baking soda and salt. In a medium-sized bowl, beat together the mashed banana, olive oil, nondairy milk, sugars, tahini and vanilla.

Add the wet ingredients to the dry and mix until just combined. Fold in the dates. Pour the batter into the prepared loaf pan and top with a generous sprinkle of sesame seeds and a pinch of flaky sea salt. Bake for 50 to 55 minutes, or until deeply golden brown and a toothpick inserted into the center comes out relatively clean. A few moist crumbs are okay.

Remove from the oven and let the banana bread cool in the pan for 15 minutes, then transfer to a wire rack. Allow to cool for at least another 20 minutes before slicing.

INDEX